Published in Great Britain in MMXXII by
Scribblers, an imprint of
The Salariya Book Company Ltd
25 Marlborough Place, Brighton BN1 1UB
www.salariya.com

ISBN: 978-1-913971-21-2

© The Salariya Book Company Ltd MMXXII
All rights reserved. No part of this publication may be reproduced, stored in or introduced into a retrieval system or transmitted in any form, or by any means (electronic, mechanical, photocopying, recording or otherwise) without the written permission of the publisher. Any person who does any unauthorised act in relation to this publication may be liable to criminal prosecution and civil claims for damages.

1 3 5 7 9 8 6 4 2

A CIP catalogue record for this book is available from the British Library.

This book is sold subject to the conditions that it shall not, by way of trade or otherwise, be lent, resold, hired out, or otherwise circulated without the publisher's prior consent in any form or binding or cover other than that in which it is published and without similar condition being imposed on the subsequent purchaser.

Editor: Nick Pierce

Visit

for our online catalogue and
free fun stuff.

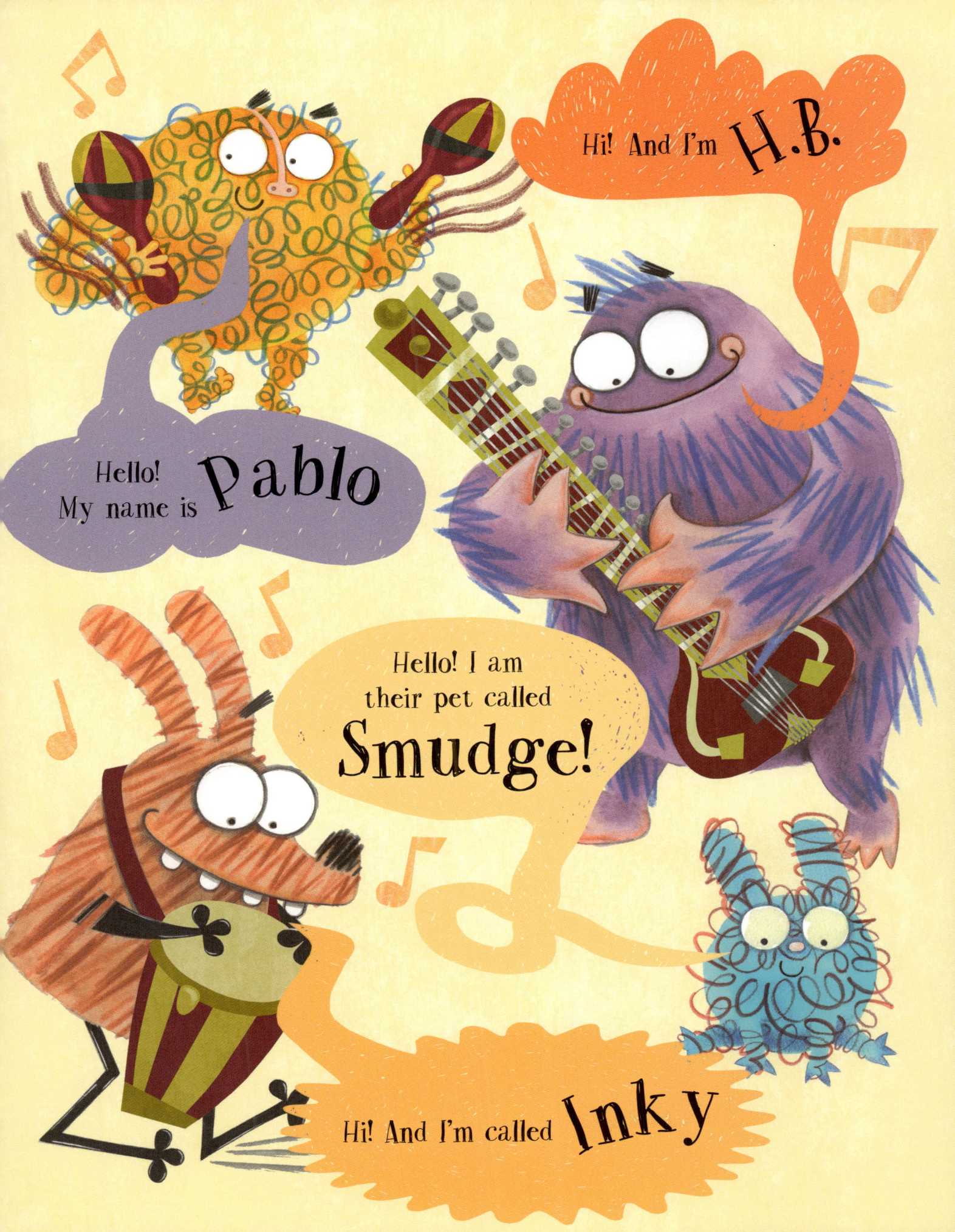

Some little children can forget
To pick up junk behind them...
We're here to scribble our advice
And find ways to remind them.

Pablo isn't very happy,
And feels a little bitter...
He slipped on a banana skin
Among a lot of litter.

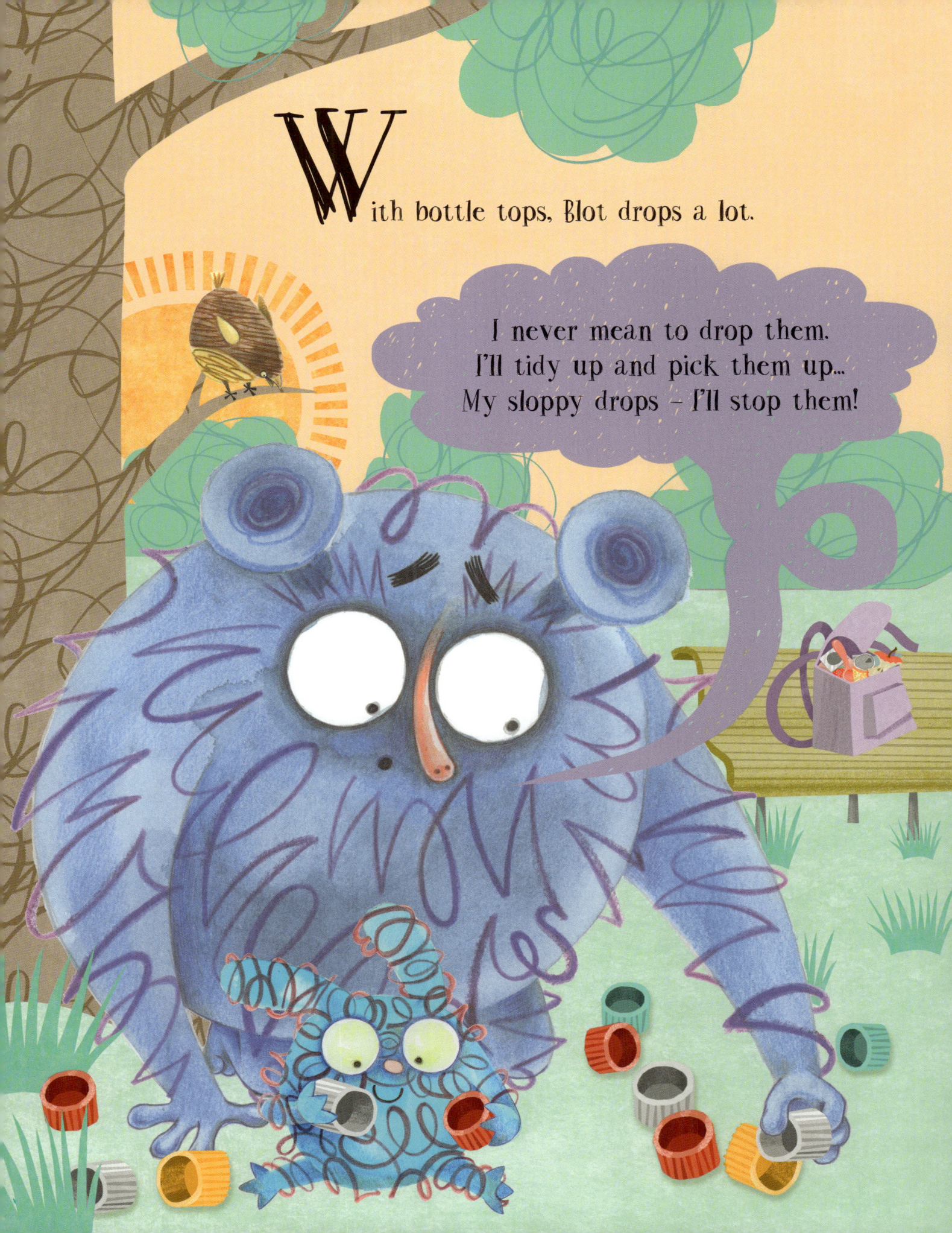

When Nibs and Smudge play in the park,
They sigh,

"No, this is wrong –
The grass is cluttered up with waste."

So they sing their **Garbage Song**...

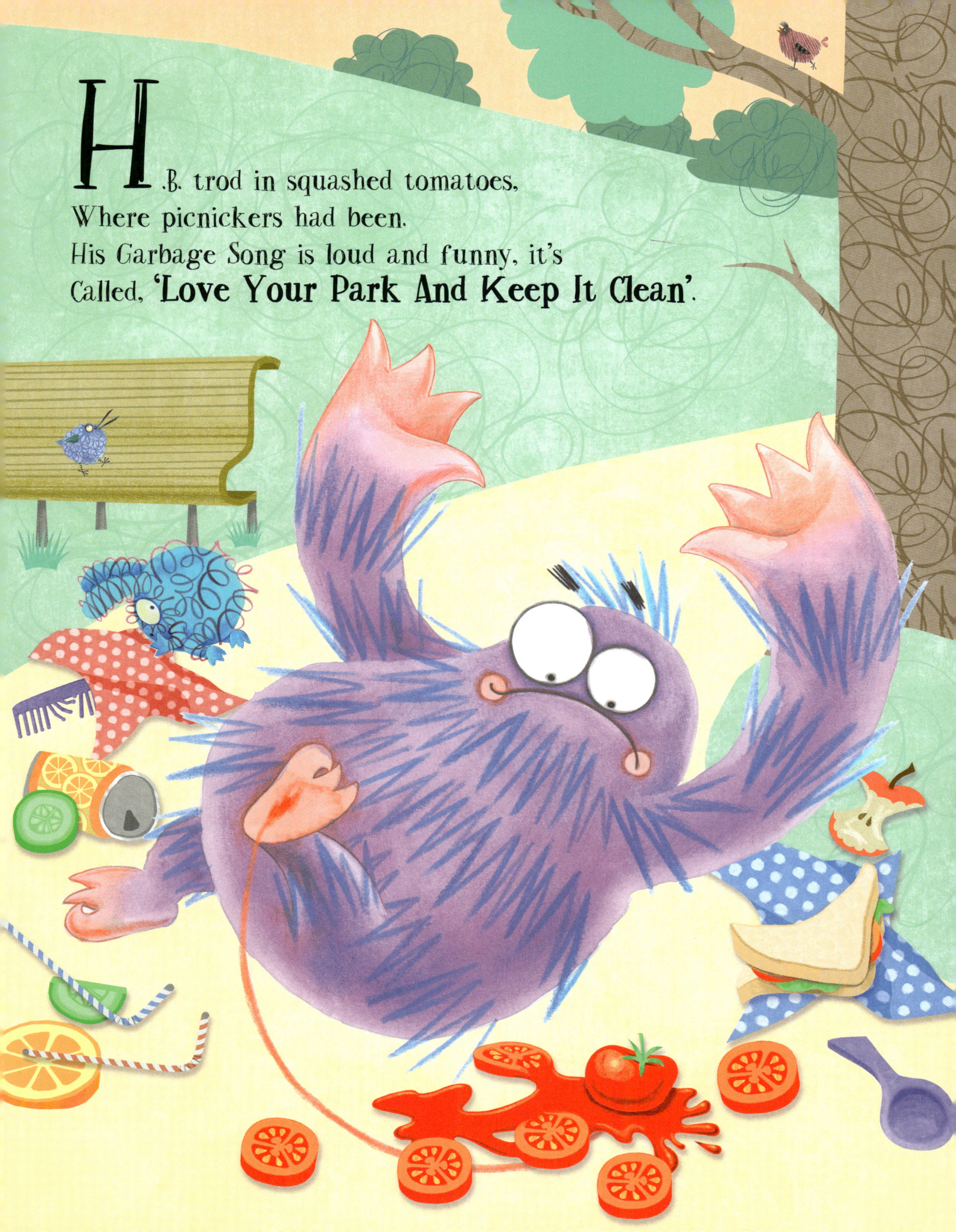

H.B. trod in squashed tomatoes,
Where picnickers had been.
His Garbage Song is loud and funny, it's
Called, **'Love Your Park And Keep It Clean'**.

Stooping down to pick up litter
Can't be hard work, can it?
That's all it needs for us to show
Good manners to our planet!

Children clearing up their garbage
Like to sing along,
To the Scribble Monsters playing
Their 'PICK UP LITTER' song.

H.B., Inky, Nibs and Pablo,
Blot and Smudge all sing...
'Don't forget to take your litter –
And that means everything!'

HAVE YOU HEARD THE MAGIC WORD?

The Scribble Monsters wave goodbye
With friendly flags and banners
To help all children to remember
Those **SCRIBBLE MONSTER MANNERS!**

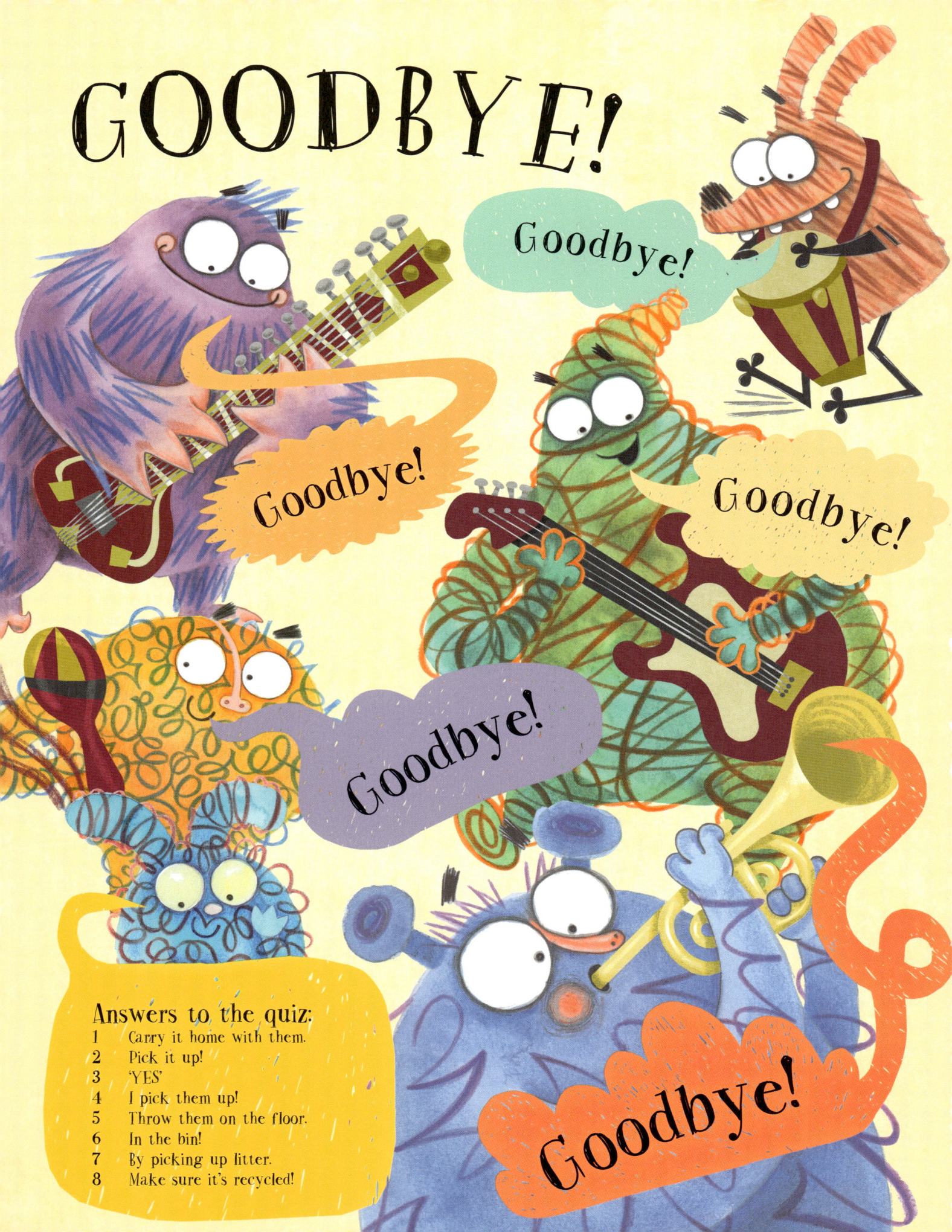